THIS IGLOO BOOK BELONGS TO:

....

igloobooks

Published in 2022
First published in the UK by Igloo Books Ltd
An imprint of Igloo Books Ltd
Cottage Farm, NN6 0BJ, UK
Owned by Bonnier Books
Sveavägen 56, Stockholm, Sweden
www.igloobooks.com

1022 001
2 4 6 8 10 9 7 5 3 1
ISBN 978-1-80108-349-2

Written by Stephanie Moss
Illustrated by Hannah Wood

Designed by Alex Alexandrou
Edited by Claire Mowat

Printed and manufactured in China

BAD FAIRY

igloobooks

The new girl
in town was
as bad as could be.

When anyone saw her,
away they would flee.

The fairies all hid,
and they blocked
up their doors...

... while she grumped and she grouched and she raged and she

ROARED!

"Why is she angry?"
they whispered in fear.

"She's been in a mood since
the day she moved here."

They thought of the rule that their elders decided
to make sure the fairies were never divided.

Be peaceful.
Be calm.
Be happy together.
Be kind, or risk
losing your
magic forever!

If things didn't change,
it could all be destroyed.
So, they asked her to yoga.

YOGA

"It might bring
you joy!"

"Be a tree, be a dog, do a warrior pose."

"Be a cow, be a cat, reach right *down* to your toes."

"Be a snail, a dragon, a lion that ROARS..."

... till Juno thought, "No, I can't do any more..."

... and cast a bad spell so they'd fall on the floor!

Could calm meditation
make Juno less bad?
But, as soon as she tried,
it just made her more mad.

She breathed in and out
from right down in her belly,
and cast a bad spell that
was terribly smelly!

Their final attempt was to look at the sky
and pick out the shapes of the clouds that passed by.
How **peaceful** and **calm** all the fairies were feeling...

... but Juno found this task the most unappealing.

Just as they drifted to sleep and relaxed,
the sky started rumbling, and then it turned...

BLACK!

"Our magic is fading.
Our powers feel low.
You're a BAD FAIRY.
We need you to go!"

In a
FLASH,
Juno left,
but her badness
had spread.

Then dark clouds of grey
appeared over their heads.

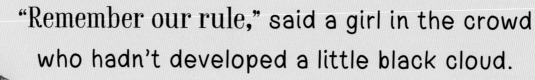

"Remember our rule," said a girl in the crowd
who hadn't developed a little black cloud.

"Be happy TOGETHER. Be kind and be calm.
We sent Juno home, and we've ALL come to harm."

"We made a mistake, and we need Juno back!"
So, they followed her home with a...

FIZZ! POP! PING! CRACK!

They arrived in the kingdom where Juno once lived
and hoped she'd agree to forget and forgive.
Instead, they discovered that Juno was...

QUEEN!

Her subjects agreed she was kind and not mean!

The fairies, befuddled,
had got it all wrong.
"Our friend's been
a good fairy all along!"

Then, with a twinkle
and flutter of wings,
Juno appeared to
explain everything.

I felt so unhappy
when I was the queen.
But leaving my home wasn't
quite what it seemed!

I'm sorry for acting
so grumpy and bad.
Without my old life,
I just felt really sad.

I missed being queen.
I had nothing to do,
but I shouldn't have
taken it all out on you.

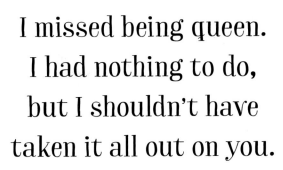

So, where's Juno now?
Do you think you can guess?
Is she living her bad life,
or one full of stress?

Neither, of course,
for the fairies come through!
"We've found you a job,
and it's PERFECT for you."

She isn't too stressed,
and she isn't too bored.
With Juno in charge,
all their magic's restored!